PLANET KINDER-GARTEN

The countdown started.

Dad and I checked the plans for my next big mission.

DAY ONE

My doctor gave me two thumbs up.

Mom and I got lots of supplies.

Today is liftoff. I suit up. Dad helps me with my gear.

"What if I am not ready? What if we crash into a comet, or get sucked into a black hole, or even worse . . . my lunch floats away?!"

"You are well prepared," says Dad.

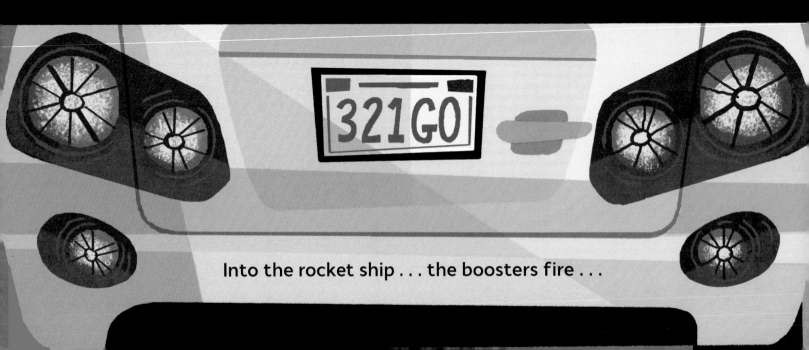

321GO

Into the rocket ship . . . the boosters fire . . .

PLANET KINDER-GARTEN

BY SUE GANZ-SCHMITT

ILLUSTRATED BY SHANE PRIGMORE

SCHOLASTIC INC.

We arrive at the base camp, then orbit
while we look for a place to dock.

I am assigned to my commander, capsule, and crewmates.

"Don't leave!" I beg.

Mom slips her photo into my pocket, and squeezes my hand.

I don't want her to worry, so I stand tall.

Parents are sent back to their own planets.

We're aliens from many galaxies on Planet Kindergarten.

Our commander tells us our flight plan for the day.

Mission control calls in on the intercom. They welcome us on our journey.

I try to get used to the new atmosphere, but it's not like home.
For one thing, gravity works differently here. We have to try hard to
stay in our seats. And our hands go up a lot.

At recess, we test the conditions outside our capsule.

A crewmate and I disagree over the equipment.

We have to sit in isolation, and I learn
that isolation isn't any fun.

My crewmate agrees, and I have a new friend.

Back in the capsule we run some experiments, write in our logs, and then capture images for our families.

I wish they were here.

At lunch, I find out that I love space food!

My lunch doesn't float away,
but our trash will, so we contain it.

The commander says that space exploration makes you tired, and we have to rest.

I am too excited to sleep, so I count stars.

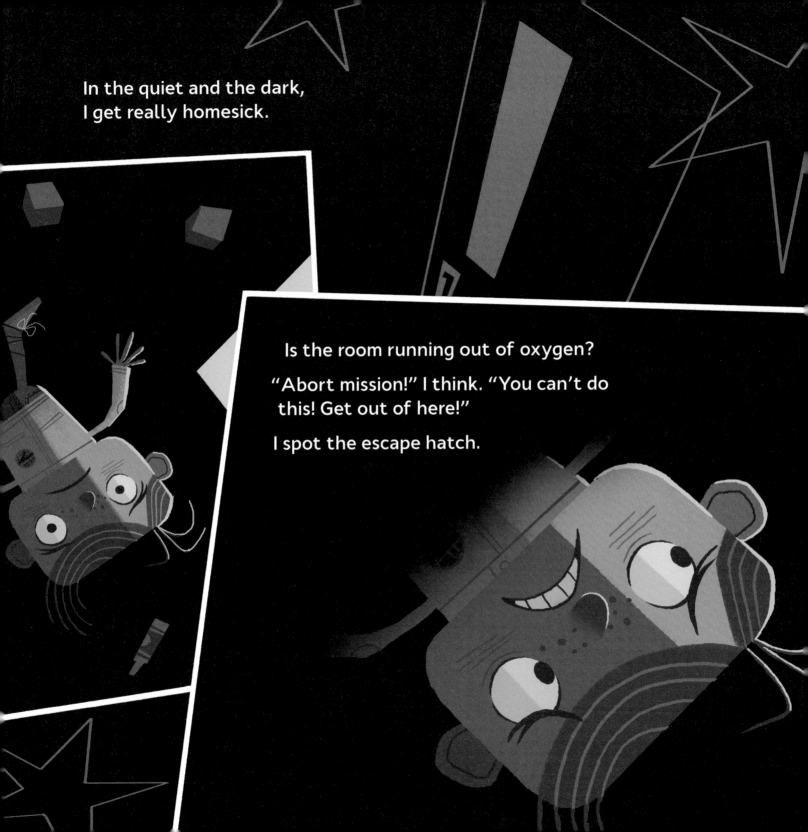

In the quiet and the dark,
I get really homesick.

Is the room running out of oxygen?

"Abort mission!" I think. "You can't do
this! Get out of here!"

I spot the escape hatch.

Then . . . I remember what they say at NASA:

FAILURE IS NOT AN OPTION.

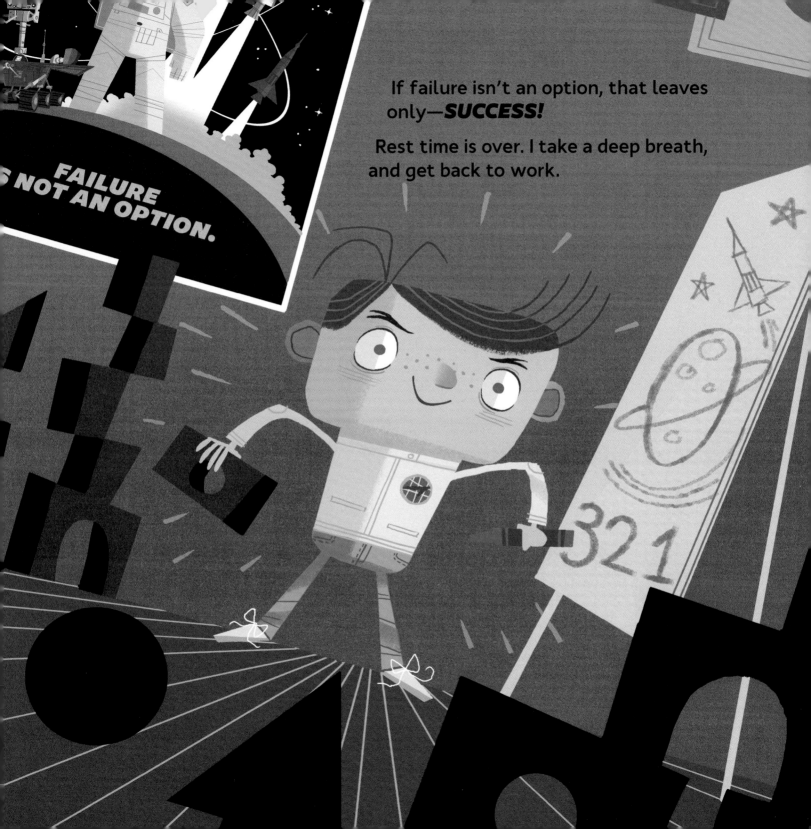

If failure isn't an option, that leaves only—**SUCCESS!**

Rest time is over. I take a deep breath, and get back to work.

FAILURE IS NOT AN OPTION.

Before I know it, my mission is accomplished!

My parents rush to greet me.

Then it's splashdown.

I am back on my home planet.

Mom and Dad are proud. Me, too, because they were brave to let me go.

I love it here, but I'm already training to go back to Planet Kindergarten tomorrow.

TO THE BRIGHT STARS TWINKLING IN MY SKY: MARTIN,
JENSEN, AND INDIA. AND TO MOM—FOR THE LOVE OF BOOKS
AND THE EXCITEMENT OF NASA ROCKET LAUNCHES. —S. G. S.

TO GIA. WELCOME TO PLANET EARTH, LITTLE ONE. —S. P.

ISBN 978-0-545-86351-3

Text copyright © 2014 by Sue Ganz-Schmitt. Illustrations copyright © 2014
by Shane Prigmore. All rights reserved. Published by Scholastic Inc.,
557 Broadway, New York, NY 10012, by arrangement with Chronicle Books LLC.
SCHOLASTIC and associated logos are trademarks and/or registered trademarks
of Scholastic Inc.

12 11 10 9 8 7 6 5 4   15 16 17 18 19 20/0

Printed in the U.S.A.   40

First Scholastic printing, April 2015

Design by Amelia May Mack
Typeset in Outage and Cyntho Pro
The illustrations in this book were rendered digitally.